MAGGIE'S
RED CIRCUS BUS

Published in 2024 by JayJayBooks
ISBN: 978-1-9163923-6-6

Written by Sue Wickstead
Illustrations by Jo Anne Davies
Layout design by Claire Shaw

MAGGIE'S
RED CIRCUS BUS

SUE WICKSTEAD

Dedicated to:

For David, who decorated the red Playbus
for the 'Circus' carnival event.

And

For Mandy, Maggie and Dennis from Ipswich.

Children waited excitedly as Maggie drove the big, bright red bus through the park gates.

Here, at last, was the new Playbus, and the children were ready to jump on board, play, and have fun.

It had taken a lot of hard work to get the Playbus ready. Maggie and her team of playworkers had planned a summer of circus fun. The bus would visit children and their families, bringing excitement to them through the summer holidays.

The bus was filled with many things the children could play with and make. There was also lots of fancy dress and face paint to use with their role-playing adventures.

BUS
STOP
DENNIS
LK59 DZH

There was only one small problem . . .

Each day, when Maggie and her team drove the red bus to its next destination, they passed adults waiting at bus stops.

When the adults saw the bus coming, they would hold out their hands, signaling their request for it to stop. But Maggie did not stop, and the people needing to go to work would watch crossly as the bus drove on by.

Maggie smiled to herself. How surprised would they be if she did stop?

There would not be many seats to sit on, and they would find the bus full of paint and toys to play with instead.

As the summer events got underway, Maggie and her team were ready to bring the circus fun to the children.

The parents had followed the schedule and knew where the bus would be every day. The children loved the Playbus visits and would run along excitedly to join in.

Over the summer, the children juggled, walked on stilts, practiced acrobatics, built play tents, and dressed up as clowns. At the end of each week, they put on performances for parents and visitors.

Dressed up in costumes and with their faces painted, the children loved sharing their work and making everyone laugh and cheer.

At the end of the summer, Maggie thought they could hold an extra special circus event to show off the skills the children had learnt in their bus groups.

The children thought this was a great idea, too. They talked non-stop about what they would do in the final event.

"I'm going to be a juggler," said one little boy as he showed his juggling skills.

"I think you are getting really good," said Maggie. "You didn't drop anything that time."

Two children were getting
really good on the stilts and
decided they would do some
stilt walking for the show.

Another boy said, "I'm going to
be a lion tamer, and my little
brother is going to be a lion."

"Roar!" said the little brother.

"Look at my cartwheels," said a little girl
   as she did a perfect tumble.

"I can do that, too," said her friend.

The girls demonstrated their cartwheels, handstands,
   and backwards rolls. Two more of their friends joined in,
   and soon, they were making up a routine. They made
   ribbon sticks to wave during their performance.

"That's very good," said Maggie. "What great
   gymnastic skills you all have. I could never
   do a cartwheel like yours."

"Maybe we could add some music with instruments," suggested one
 of the girls.

"We could learn a few songs, too!" the children said.

"A drum roll, please," said the gymnastics group.

They performed their cartwheels again to the beat of the drum,
 adding a bow as they finished.

"We're going to be clowns," said a boy and his little sister.

They pretended to throw a bucket of water at Maggie,
but it was only full of confetti.

Maggie laughed.

"We could blow a few bubbles," said a little boy.
"Everyone loves bubbles."

Maggie smiled. "That's a good idea."

The children decided they would need a ringmaster—someone
who should be in charge.

"David would be good," the children suggested. "He's good
at organising."

"You will need to keep everyone in order, David," said Maggie.

He puffed out his chest and smiled proudly. "I'm sure I can
do that."

Maggie found some animal hats in the dressing-up box for the littlest children. They could join in with the performers whenever they could.

The gymnastics crew did backbends and made an arch for the littlest children to crawl through. With roly-poly forward rolls and dancing, they giggled and had lots of fun.

Maggie was delighted when she found out the Lady Mayor would officially open the bus.

The children were even more excited. They painted pictures and made posters to advertise the event.

It was almost the day of the final circus event. The windows were decorated with different circus performers smiling out from the bus. They had made brightly coloured flags and bunting and had balloons ready, too.

The children had rehearsed their acts in costumes and makeup.

The plain red bus needed to dress up, too. But how could they make it stand out?

Maggie had an idea. She asked the parents and children to bring some big cardboard boxes from home the next day.

The next morning, Maggie was surprised to see all the different boxes the families had managed to find. The children helped her cut out large letters from the boxes to go along the sides of the bus.

"Paint the letters in many different colours," she told the children.

"Make them bright like a rainbow."

The children painted each letter as they talked about the final event. They were excited but also a little nervous.

"What if I drop the juggling balls?"

"What if I fall off my stilts?"

"Don't worry," said David. "I will be in charge. You will be fine."

With all of the letters painted and dried, Maggie set a ladder next to the Playbus. The children passed her the decorations so she could fix them to the sides of the bus.

The letters spelt 'PLAYBUS.' Now, everyone would know exactly what the charming bus was for.

The next day, with everything on board, Maggie drove the bus to the venue to get it prepared for the event. As she arrived, Maggie was pleased to see the children all ready to help.

But, oh no! Some of the letters had fallen off.

"No worries!" said Maggie.

She quickly cut out new letters for the children to paint and add to the side of the bus.

Phew!

With the bus now decorated with bunting, flags, and balloons fluttering in the breeze, it was time to get the children and families organised, too.

With faces painted and the children in their costumes, they practiced their performances one last time.

David was standing by to open the show. He was nervous. "Ladies and gentlemen, welcome to our big top adventure," he announced. The children began to perform. There were 'Oohs!' and 'Ahhs!' and applause and laughter.

The day was a great success, and everyone loved seeing what the children learned over the summer.

Then, it was time for the Lady Mayor to make her speech. She praised the children for their performances and thanked Maggie and her helpers for all of their hard work.

The Mayoress announced, "We have arranged for the bus to get a special paintwork. Then there will be no doubt this is a Playbus."

The ribbon was cut, and the Playbus was officially open. Everyone clapped and cheered.

PLAYBUS
BUS STOP

A month later, Maggie drove the newly decorated Playbus to
the children.

The outside had been painted with circus pictures, including
a bus stop sign with a circus tent.

"It looks just like our show," David said.

Maggie smiled and said, "The ringmaster certainly looks
like you, David."

Everyone agreed it was a great reminder of their circus adventure.

Maggie and her team drove the new bus each day. People waiting at bus stops held out their hands to request it to stop.

When Maggie drove by without stopping, the people were no longer cross. They smiled and waved, knowing this Playbus was off to entertain children.

Maggie would smile to herself, too.

PLAYBUS
DENNIS
LK59 DZH
BUS
STOP

THE REAL
CIRCUS PLAYBUS

We were due to take part in 'The Circus' carnival, but had only just received our new, undecorated bus – our old one was breaking down – so we needed some quick and impromptu decoration.

Sue's brother, David, cut out the letters, 'Bewbush Playbus', from cardboard boxes, and the children painted them. These letters were attached to the side of the bus with tape, but on arrival at the carnival's meeting place the 'E' had dropped off! It was a good job the bus was so well equipped with craft supplies, as we had to quickly make another one.

We were delighted that our bus won second prize!

Books by Sue Wickstead

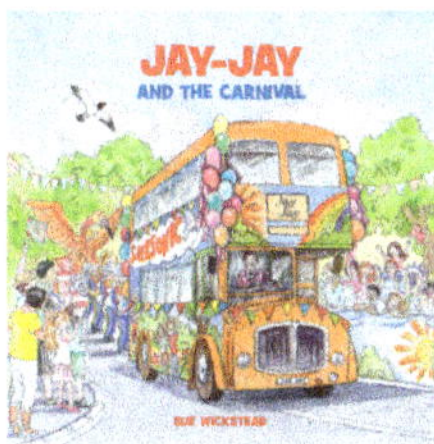
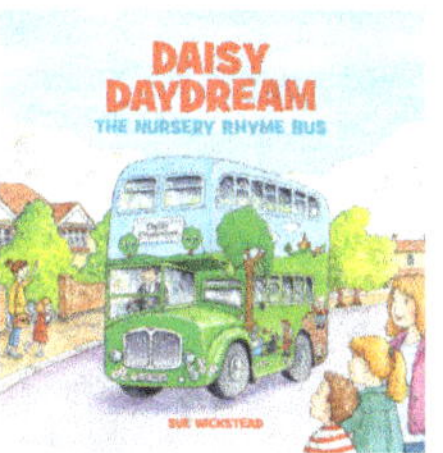
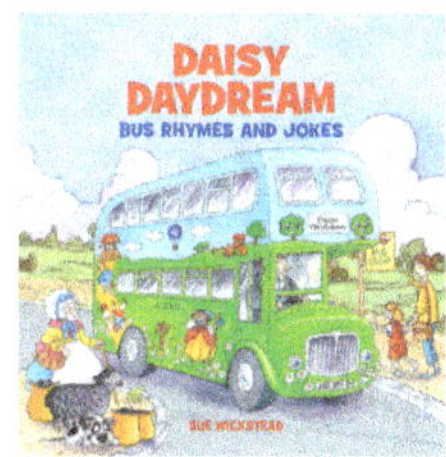

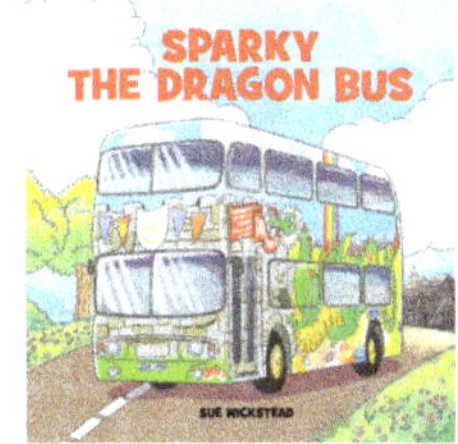

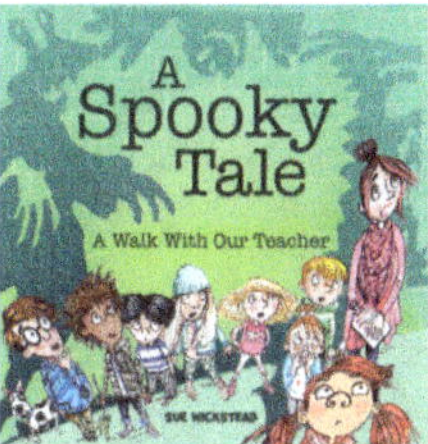

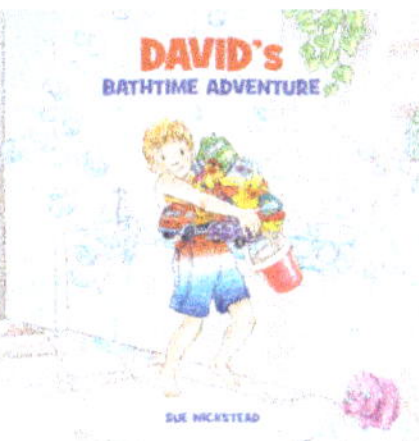
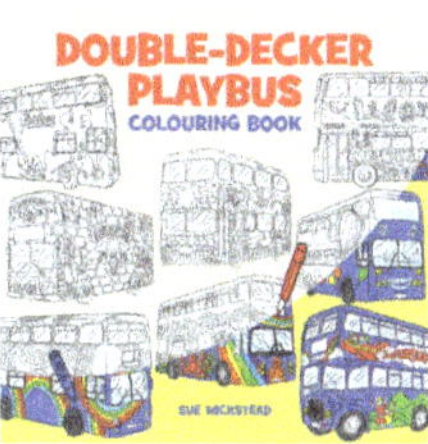

Award-winning author – 'The Wishing Shelf Book Awards'

Sue Wickstead is an author and Primary School teacher working across Sussex and Surrey. For over twenty years, alongside her teaching career, she has worked with a children's charity, The Bewbush Playbus Association, which inspired the Jay-Jay series of books. **www.suewickstead.co.uk**